Barbie™ i can be...

A Computer Engineer

Concept developed for Mattel by Egmont Creative Center
By Susan Marenco based on plots written by Giulia Conti
Illustrated by Tino Santanach & Joaquin Canizares with Pamela Duarte

Random House New York

Published in the United States by Random House Children's Books, a division of Random House, Inc., 1745 Broadway, New York, NY 10019, and in Canada by Random House of Canada Limited, Toronto.

ISBN: 978-0-449-81619-6
randomhouse.com/kids MANUFACTURED IN CHINA 10 9 8 7 6 5 4 3 2 1

At breakfast one morning, Barbie is already hard at work on her laptop.

"What are you doing, Barbie?" asks Skipper.

"I'm designing a game that shows kids how computers work," explains Barbie. "You can make a robot puppy do cute tricks by matching up colored blocks!"

"Your robot puppy is so sweet," says Skipper. "Can I play your game?"

"I'm only creating the design ideas," Barbie says, laughing. "I'll need Steven's and Brian's help to turn it into a real game!"

Barbie tries to email her design to Steven, but suddenly her screen starts blinking.

"That's weird!" says Barbie.

Barbie and Skipper try to reboot the computer, but nothing happens.

"Looks like you've got a virus, big sister," says Skipper.

"Luckily, I wear my flash drive on a necklace so that I'll always remember to back up my work," replies Barbie.

“May I borrow your laptop, Skipper?” asks Barbie as she follows her little sister into her bedroom.

“I really should finish my homework assignment. I am writing about a person I admire,” says Skipper.

“I only need it for a minute,” adds Barbie.

“Okay,” says Skipper.

When Barbie puts her flash drive into Skipper's laptop, the screen starts blinking.

"Oh, no!" says Barbie. "The virus must be on the flash drive!"

"I forgot to back up my homework assignment!" cries Skipper. "And all my music files are lost, too!"

“I’m so sorry, Skipper,” says Barbie. “I have to run off to school now. But I promise to find a way to fix your laptop.”

“You better!” Skipper replies as she playfully hits Barbie with a pillow.

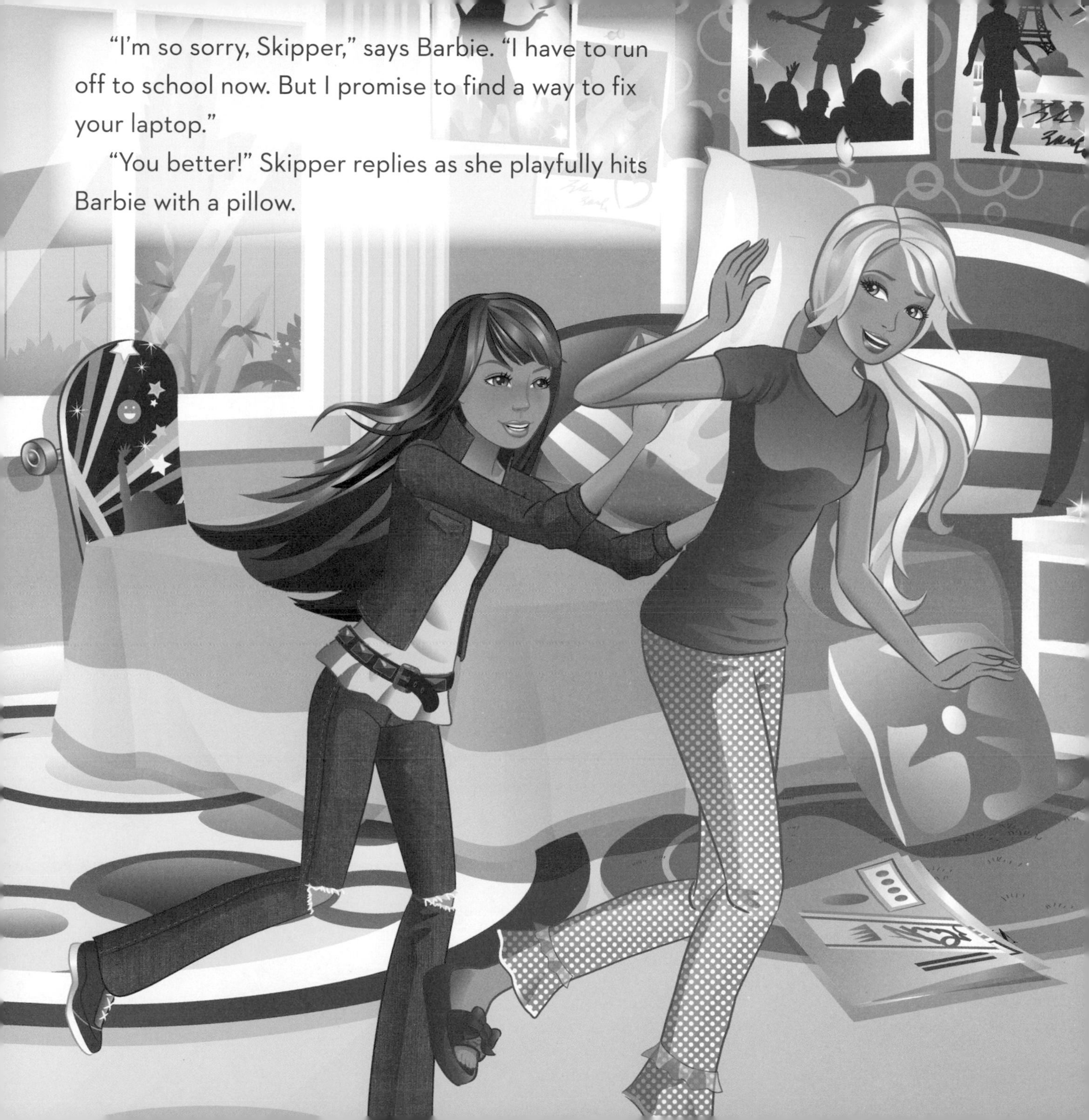

Barbie makes it to computer class just before the bell rings. As soon as class begins, Barbie raises her hand.

"Yes, Barbie?" asks Ms. Smith, the teacher.

"If your computer gets a virus and crashes, how can you retrieve all the files you lost?" asks Barbie.

"Well, first you remove the hard drive from the crashed computer," explains Ms. Smith. "And then you hook it up to another computer."

"But won't the other computer get the same virus that made your computer crash?" asks Barbie.

"Not if the computer has good security software installed," says Ms. Smith. "Good security software protects your computer from catching a virus."

After class, Barbie meets with Steven and Brian in the library.

"Hi, guys," says Barbie. "I tried to send you my designs, but I ended up crashing my laptop—and Skipper's, too! I need to get back the lost files and repair both of our laptops."

"It will go faster if Brian and I help," offers Steven.

"Great!" says Barbie. "Steven, can you hook Skipper's hard drive up to the library's computer?"

"Sure!" says Steven. "The library computer has excellent security software to protect it."

"I've got Skipper's assignment from the hard drive!" exclaims Steven.

"Fantastic!" says Barbie. "And her other files, as well?"

"I've got everything," says Steven. "Now let's retrieve the files from your hard drive. Both laptops will be good as new in no time!"

The next morning, Barbie gives her sister a big surprise. Skipper turns on her laptop—and it works!

"My lost assignment!" cries Skipper. "You are just too cool, Barbie! You fixed my computer *and* saved my homework!"

Skipper gives Barbie a huge hug.

Barbie

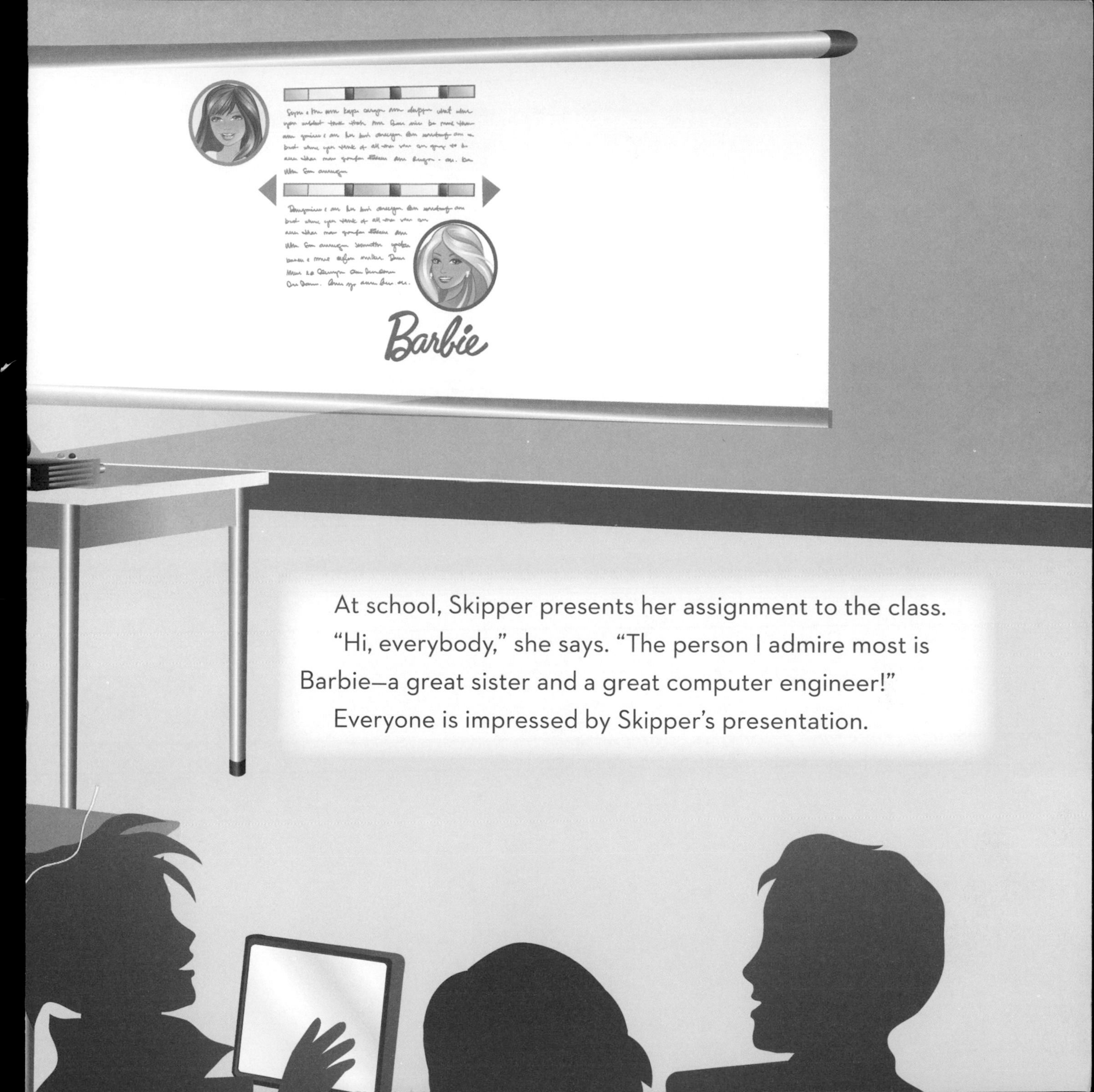

At school, Skipper presents her assignment to the class.

"Hi, everybody," she says. "The person I admire most is Barbie—a great sister and a great computer engineer!"

Everyone is impressed by Skipper's presentation.

At computer class, Barbie presents the game she designed. Ms. Smith is so impressed that she gives Barbie extra credit!

Barbie's terrific computer skills have saved the day for both sisters!

"I guess I can be a computer engineer!" says Barbie happily.

FABGirl
Barbie
© Mattel

NERDY
is the
New
FAB!
Barbie
© Mattel

DREAM
BiG
Barbie
© Mattel

© Mattel

© Mattel

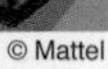
© Mattel

VIP
Barbie
ADMIT ONE
VIP
© Mattel

ADMIT ONE
VIP
ONE
Barbie
i can be...
TM
© Mattel

© Mattel
Barbie
i can be...
© Mattel
I
Barbie
© Mattel
FASHION
HISTORY
PHOTOGRAPHY
© Mattel
© Mattel
© Mattel
Barbie
© Mattel
DREAM BiG
© Mattel

Backstage, everyone congratulates Barbie on her good work.

"I guess I can be an actress—even without knowing my lines perfectly!" says Barbie.

"You were great!" says Chelsea.

"Thanks, Chelsea," says Barbie. "And you just might be an actress one day, too!"

After the final scene, the audience claps and cheers. Benjamin turns to Barbie. "I'm sorry that I fell," he says.

"No, it was *perfect*! The audience loved it!" says Barbie.

"Thanks to you, Barbie!" says Benjamin with a smile.

From backstage, Barbie and Chelsea watch Olivia play the queen.

"Onstage in fifteen seconds, Barbie," says the director. "Just say your lines like a delicate princess would if she slept in an uncomfortable bed!"

"I'll try my best," says Barbie.

"You are going to make a great princess, Barbie," says Chelsea.

"Thanks, Chelsea," says Barbie, giving her little sister a hug.

“But what if I forget a line?” asks Olivia.

“We can help each other,” says Barbie. “Just relax and have fun!”

“Thanks, Barbie,” says Olivia as she heads out to the stage.

“There’s a TV crew outside!” exclaims Chelsea.

“They make me nervous,” says Olivia.

“Don’t think about the camera,” says Barbie. “Just think about the story we’re telling.”

“But I don’t know the lines,” says Barbie.

“You know the story,” Chelsea tells her sister.

“You are a fantastic actress, Barbie,” says the director of the play. “Just answer the other actors as a real princess would.”

Everyone looks at Barbie hopefully.

“Okay, I’ll give it a try!” replies Barbie. Everyone is thrilled to have Barbie in the play!

The director also asks Chelsea to play the prince’s little sister!

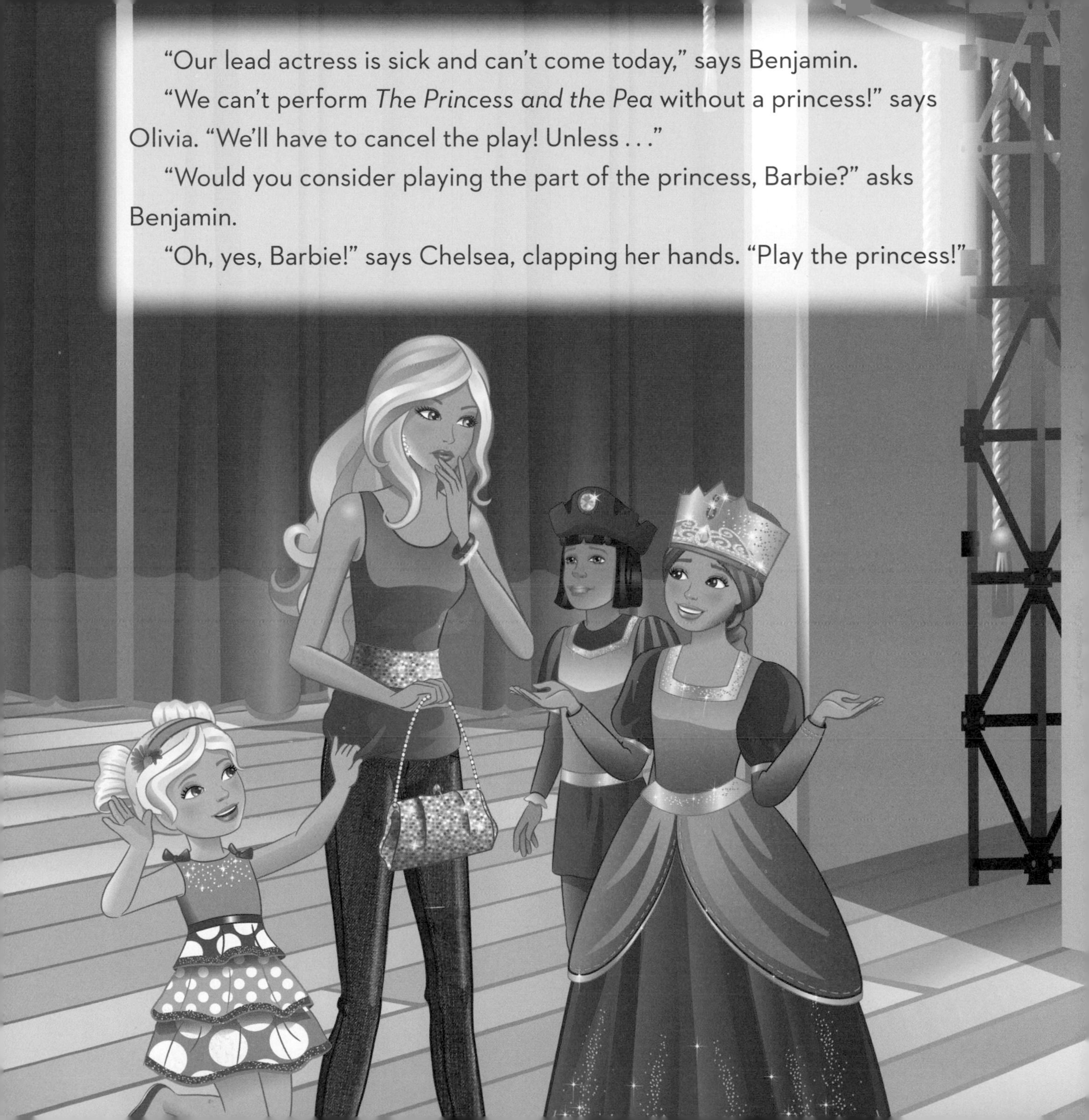

"Our lead actress is sick and can't come today," says Benjamin.

"We can't perform *The Princess and the Pea* without a princess!" says Olivia. "We'll have to cancel the play! Unless . . ."

"Would you consider playing the part of the princess, Barbie?" asks Benjamin.

"Oh, yes, Barbie!" says Chelsea, clapping her hands. "Play the princess!"

As Barbie signs a few autographs in the audience, Chelsea looks up at the stage. “Why isn’t the play starting?” she asks.

Just then, Olivia pokes her head from behind the curtain and motions to Barbie and Chelsea to come backstage.

At the mall, Barbie and Chelsea pass by a theater group getting ready to present a play. The theater actors recognize Barbie from her movies.

"Hi, Barbie," says a girl dressed in costume. "I'm Olivia, and I'm playing the queen in *The Princess and the Pea*."

"I'm playing the prince," says a boy named Benjamin. "Would you like to stay and watch us perform?"

"Sure," says Barbie. "We'd love to!"

Barbie is so excited about her next movie! She wants to learn her part perfectly, so she practices her lines in front of her little sister Chelsea.

"Can we go out somewhere, Barbie?" asks Chelsea after a few hours.

"I guess I have studied my lines enough for today," says Barbie as she hops up off the sofa. "Let's go to the mall!"

"Yippee!" says Chelsea.

An Actress

Concept developed for Mattel by Egmont Creative Center
By Susan Marenco based on plots written by Giulia Conti
Illustrated by Tino Santanach & Joaquin Canizares

Random House New York

Published in the United States by Random House Children's Books, a division of Random House, Inc., 1745 Broadway, New York, NY 10019, and in Canada by Random House of Canada Limited, Toronto.

ISBN: 978-0-449-81619-6
randomhouse.com/kids MANUFACTURED IN CHINA 10 9 8 7 6 5 4 3 2 1